One Very Best Valentine's Day

by Joan W. Blos

illustrated by Emily Arnold McCully

LITTLE SIMON
Published by Simon & Schuster
New York   London   Toronto   Sydney   Tokyo   Singapore

LITTLE SIMON
Simon & Schuster Building, Rockefeller Center,
1230 Avenue of the Americas, New York, New York 10020

LITTLE SIMON and colophon are trademarks of Simon & Schuster.
Also available in a SIMON & SCHUSTER BOOKS FOR YOUNG READERS
hardcover edition.

Manufactured in the United States of America

10   9   8   7   6   5   4   3   2

ISBN: 0-671-75297-9 (pbk)
ISBN: 0-671-64639-7

Barbara's bracelet was made of hearts
of many different colors. The hearts were attached
to one another by a stretchy string.

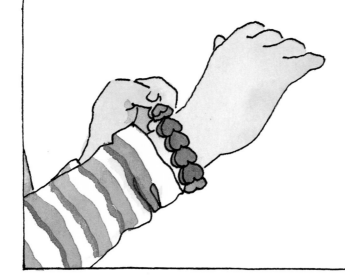

Barbara liked to snap her bracelet
and say the colors' names.
 "Red," she would say, "and blue
and yellow and purple. And orange
and light green."

One day she only got as far as yellow
when *snap!* the stretchy elastic broke,
and the hearts flew out all over.

At first they were easy to find.

A red heart
was under the rocking chair.

A blue one
was near the table.

A purple heart was caught in a leafy plant,
and the two orange hearts ended up together
at the edge of a furry rug.

Barbara collected these five hearts
together, then she hunted around
some more.

It was hard to see the blue one in the
chair that was nearly the same color.

And she had to stretch herself way out
to reach the green heart standing on its side
underneath the desk.

Even when she had gotten every one of the hearts
it was hard to remember the bracelet they had been.

When she woke up next morning,
Barbara had an idea. The idea would be
a secret for a while—something she
would not tell.

Even when her mother asked,
"Where is your bracelet, Barbara?"
Barbara said, "It's something that
I know but I cannot tell."

Even when her brothers asked,
she did not tell them anything.

Or her father or her aunt.

Barbara kept her secret
until it was Valentine's Day.

Then, there were presents for everyone
made from Barbara's bracelet. So Barbara
didn't have her bracelet anymore,
and she didn't have her secret.

But they all liked their surprises,
and they all had a very good time.
And that is exactly what happened
one very best Valentine's Day.